GULEESH

A Picture Story from Ireland

ISBN	0-695-80036-1	Trade binding
ISBN	0-695-40036-3	Titan binding

Library of Congress Catalog Card Number: 77-165545

First Printing

Guleesh

A PICTURE STORY FROM IRELAND

ILLUSTRATED BY
WILLIAM STOBBS
Text from Joseph Jacobs

FOLLETT PUBLISHING COMPANY / CHICAGO

THERE was once a boy in the County Mayo; Guleesh was his name. There was the finest rath a little way off from the gable of the house, and he was often in the habit of seating himself on the fine grass bank at the edge of the trees. One November night he stood watching the beautiful white moon over his head, and he said to himself: "I'd sooner be any place in the world than here. Och, it's well for you, white moon that's turning around as you please yourself. I wish I was as free as you."

Hardly was the word out of his mouth when he heard a great noise coming like the sound of many people running together and talking and laughing and making sport. And the sound went by him like a whirl of wind.

What was in it but the fairy host, and he followed the little *sheehogues* into the rath. There he heard every man of them crying out as loud as he could: “My horse and bridle and saddle! My horse and bridle and saddle!”

“By my hand,” said Guleesh, “I’ll imitate ye,” and he cried out as well as they: “My horse and bridle and saddle! My horse and bridle and saddle!” And on the moment there was a fine horse with a bridle of gold and a saddle of silver standing before him. He leaped up on it, and the moment he was on its back he saw clearly that the rath was full of horses, and of little people going riding on them.

"Are you coming with us tonight, Guleesh?" said one of the sheehogues.

"I am surely," said Guleesh.

And out they went all together, riding like the wind, faster than the fastest horse ever you saw a-hunting, and faster than the fox and the hounds at his tail. And stop nor stay did they make none, until they came to the brink of the sea.

Then every one of them said: "Hie over cap! Hie over cap!" and that moment they were up in the air, and before Guleesh had time to remember where he was, they were down on dry land again, going like the wind until at last they stood still.

"You're in France, Guleesh," said one of the little men. "The daughter of the king of France is to be married tonight, the handsomest woman that the sun ever saw, and we must do our best to bring her with us. You must come with us that we may put the young girl up behind you on the horse, for it's not lawful for us to put her sitting behind ourselves."

They got off their horses, and a man of them said a word that Guleesh did not understand, and on the moment Guleesh found himself and his companions in the palace. A great feast was going on there, and the night was as bright as the day with all the lamps and candles that were lit. The musicians were playing the sweetest music that ever a man's ear heard, and there were young women and fine youths in the middle of the hall, dancing and turning. The old king had only the one daughter, and she was to be married to the son of another king that night.

Guleesh and his companions were standing together at the head of the hall, where there was a fine altar and two bishops waiting to marry the girl. Now nobody could see the sheehogues, for they said a word as they came in that made them all invisible.

Guleesh looked about the hall, and there he saw the loveliest woman that ever was upon the ridge of the world. The rose and the lily were fighting together in her face, and one could not tell which of them got the victory. Her garments and dress were woven with gold and silver, and the bright stone that was in the ring on her hand was as shining as the sun. But Guleesh saw that there was the trace of tears in her eyes.

"She is grieved," said one sheehogue, "for she has no love for the husband she is to marry. It's time for her to marry; but, indeed, it's no king's son she'll marry, if we can help it."

Guleesh pitied the young lady, and was heartbroken to think that she must marry a man she did not like, or what was worse, take a sheehogue for a husband.

When the dancing was over, the girl's father and mother came up and said that this was the right time to put the wedding ring on her and give her to her husband. The king took the youth by the hand, and the queen took her daughter, and they went up together to the altar, with the lords and great people following them.

When they came near the altar, one sheehogue stretched out his foot before the girl, and she fell. Before she was able to rise again, he threw something that was in his hand upon her, said a couple of words, and upon the moment the maiden was made invisible. The sheehogues seized her, and out of the door of the palace they went, without being stopped or hindered, for nobody could see them.

"My horse, my bridle, and saddle!" said every man of them.

"My horse, my bridle, and saddle!" said Guleesh; and on the moment the horse was standing ready before him. Guleesh raised the girl up on the horse's back, leaped up himself, and, "Rise, horse," said he. Then his horse, and the other horses with him, went in a full race until they came to the sea.

"Hie over cap!" said every man of them.

"Hie over cap!" said Guleesh; and on the moment the horse rose under him, cut a leap in the clouds, and came down in Erin. They did not stop there, but went to the place where was Guleesh's house and the rath.

And when they came as far as that, Guleesh turned and caught the young girl in his two arms, and leaped off the horse.

"I call and cross you to myself, in the name of God!" said he. And on the spot, before the word was out of his mouth, the horse fell down, and what was in it but the beam of a plow, from which the sheehogues had made a horse. And every other horse they had, it returned to the thing from which they had made it. Some of them were riding on an old besom, and some on a broken stick, and more on a *bohalawn* or a hemlock stalk.

"O, Guleesh, isn't that a nice turn you did us, and we so kind to you?" the little people called out together. "Never mind yet, you clown, you'll pay us another time for this." But they had no power to carry off the girl now that Guleesh had spoken his vow.

"He'll have no good to get out of that girl," said the little man who had talked to Guleesh in the palace, and he struck her a slap on the side of the head. "Now," said he, "she'll be without talk anymore. Guleesh, what good will she be to you when she'll be dumb? It's time for us to go—but you'll remember us, Guleesh!"

When he said that, he stretched out his two hands, and before Guleesh was able to give an answer, he and the rest of them were gone into the rath out of his sight.

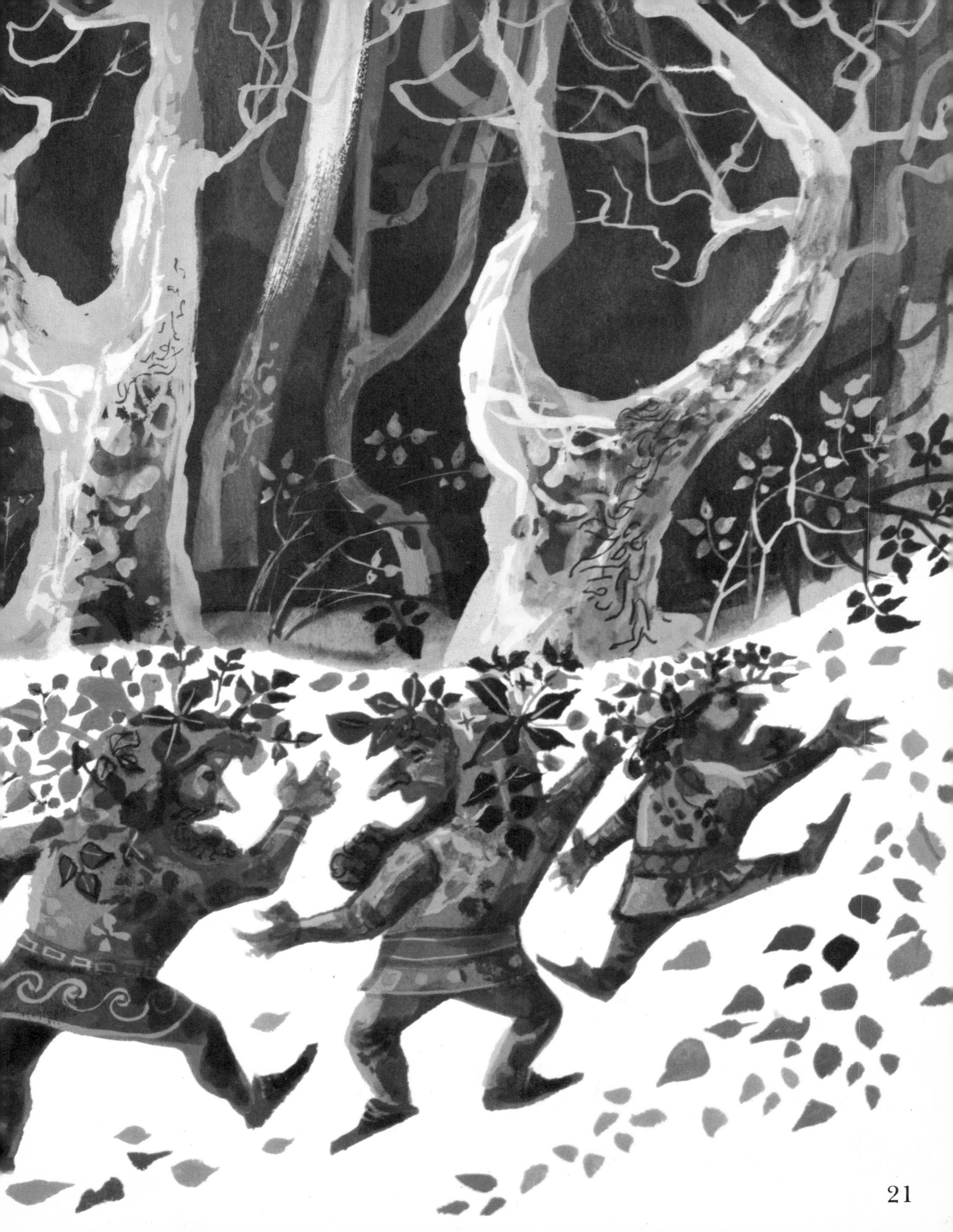

"Lady," said Guleesh, "tell me what you would like me to do now. I never belonged at all to that lot of sheehogues who carried you away. I am the son of an honest farmer, and I went with them without knowing what they planned. If ever I'm able to send you back to your father, I'll do it."

The girl raised her white smooth hand and laid her finger on her tongue to show him that she had lost her voice and power of speech, and the tears ran out of her two eyes.

Guleesh did not like to bring her home to his father's house, for he knew well that they would not believe who she was.

"I know what I'll do," said he. "I'll bring her to the priest's house." And so they went, and as early as it was, the priest was up and opened the door himself.

"Guleesh, Guleesh, isn't it the nice boy you are that you can't wait till ten o'clock or till twelve, but that you must be coming to me at this hour, looking for marriage, you and your sweetheart?"

"Father," said Guleesh, "it's not looking for marriage I came to you now, but to ask you, if you please, to give a lodging in your house to this young lady."

The priest looked at him as though he had ten heads on him, but without putting any other question, he desired them to come in.

“Now, Guleesh,” said he, “tell me truly who is this young lady?”

“I’m not telling a word of lie,” said Guleesh; “she is the daughter of the king of France.”

He told the whole to the priest then, and said that he would be very thankful if the priest would keep her in his own house. The kind man said he would do that, because they had no means of sending her back to her father again.

The days passed, and seldom one went by but Guleesh would go to the priest’s house and hope to find the young lady well again. But, alas! She remained silent.

She carried on a sort of conversation by moving her hands and fingers, laughing or smiling, and giving a thousand other signs, so that it was not long until they understood each other very well. This was the way they were for many months, and Guleesh was falling deeper and deeper in love with her every day.

So they passed the time for a year, until there came a day when Guleesh remembered that it was the same November night a year ago when the whirlwind came, and the sheehogues in it, and he said to himself: "We have November night again tonight, and I'll stand in the same place until I see if the little people come again."

So Guleesh went to the old rath and stood, waiting. The moon rose slowly. There was no sound to be heard but the *cronawn* of the insects that would go by from time to time, or the hoarse sudden scream of the wild geese, or the sharp whistle of the golden plover, rising and lying, lying and rising, as they do on a calm night. There were a thousand thousand bright stars shining over his head.

He was beginning to think that the sheehogues would not come that night, and that it was as good for him to go back again, when he heard a sound far away, coming toward him. The sound increased, and at first it was like the beating of waves on a stony shore, and then it was like the falling of a great waterfall, and at last it was like a loud storm in the tops of the trees, and then the whirlwind burst into the rath, and the sheehogues were in it.

Scarcely had they gathered in the rath till they all began shouting and screaming and talking among themselves. And then each one of them cried out: "My horse and bridle and saddle! My horse and bridle and saddle!"

Guleesh took courage and called out as loudly as any of them: "My horse and bridle and saddle!"

But before the word was well out of his mouth, one little man cried out: "Guleesh, my boy, are you here with us again? There's no use in your calling for your horse tonight. You won't play such a trick on us again."

"Isn't he a prime lad, to take a woman with him that never said as much as 'How do you do?' since this time last year!" said a second sheehogue.

"And if he only knew that there's an herb growing up by his own door, and if he were to boil it and give it to her, she'd be well," said a third.

And with that they rose up into the air and left poor Guleesh looking after them and wondering.

"It can't be," said Guleesh to himself, "that they would tell me of the herb if there was any virtue in it. But perhaps the sheehogue didn't observe himself when he let the word slip out of his mouth."

So Guleesh went home, and the first thing he did was to search well through the grass around the house. He was not long searching till he observed a large strange herb growing just by the door. He cut the plant and put it in a little pot with a little water in it, and laid it on the fire until the water was boiling. Then he raised a couple of drops on the tip of his finger and put it to his mouth. It was not bitter, and, indeed, had a sweet, agreeable taste. He grew bolder then and drank till he had half the cup drunk. After that he fell asleep and did not wake for hours and hours.

As soon as he got up, he went to the priest's house with the drink in his hand. He found the priest and the young lady within and told them all his news. Guleesh handed her the cup, and she drank half of it, and then fell back on the bed. A heavy sleep came on her, and she never woke till the day on the morrow.

The two men were in great anxiety waiting to see whether she would speak. When her eyes were finally open, the priest said to her: "Did you sleep well?"

And she answered him: "I slept, thank you."

No sooner did Guleesh hear her talking than he fell on his two knees and said: "A thousand thanks to God, who has given you back the talk, lady of my heart."

After that Guleesh used to come to the priest's house from day to day, and the friendship that was between him and the king's daughter increased.

So they married one another, and it was a fine wedding they had. And if I had been there then, I would not be here now; but I heard it from a birdeen that there was neither cark nor care, sickness nor sorrow, mishap nor misfortune on them till the hour of their death, and may the same be with me, and with us all!

DATE DUE